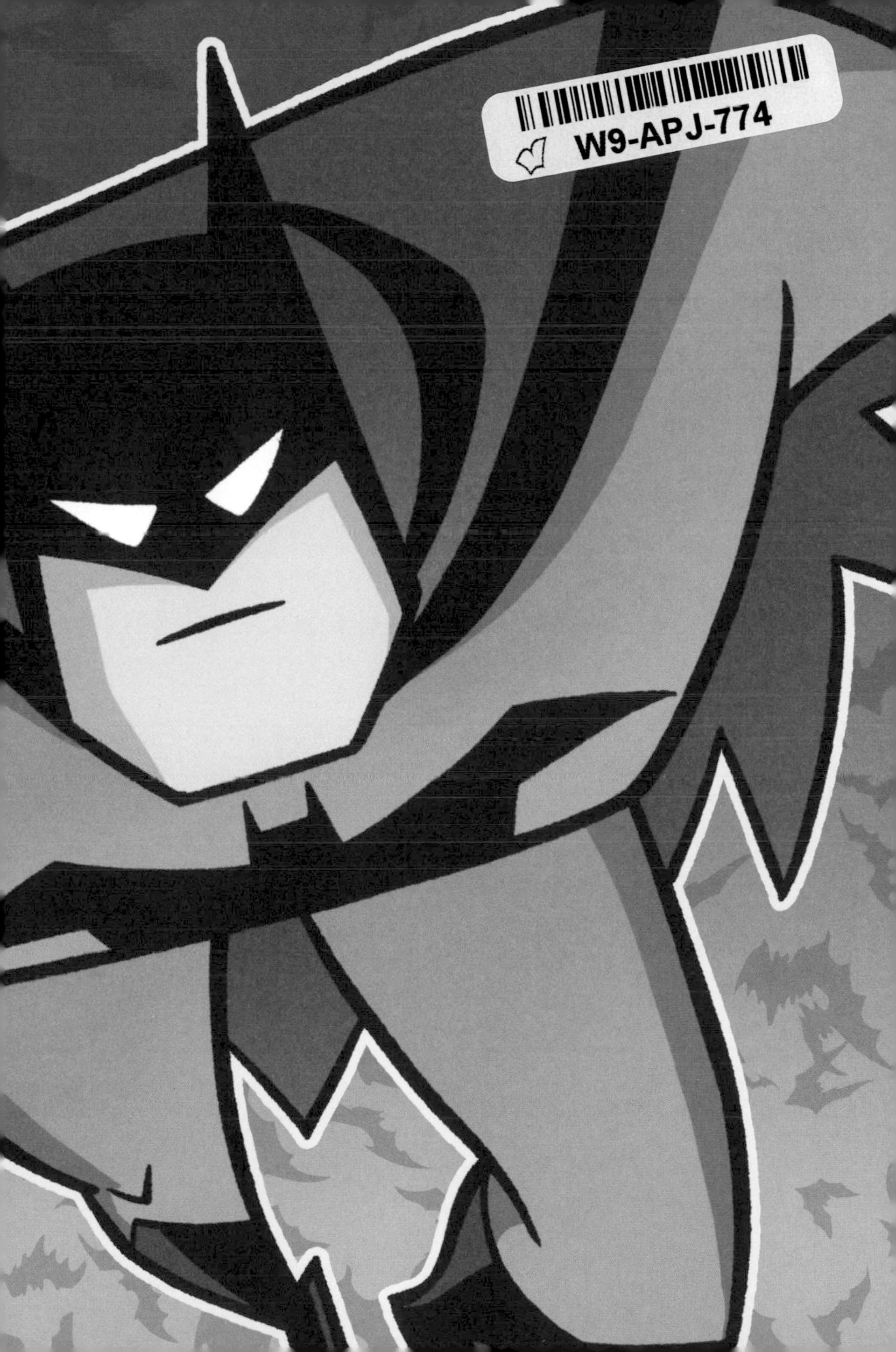

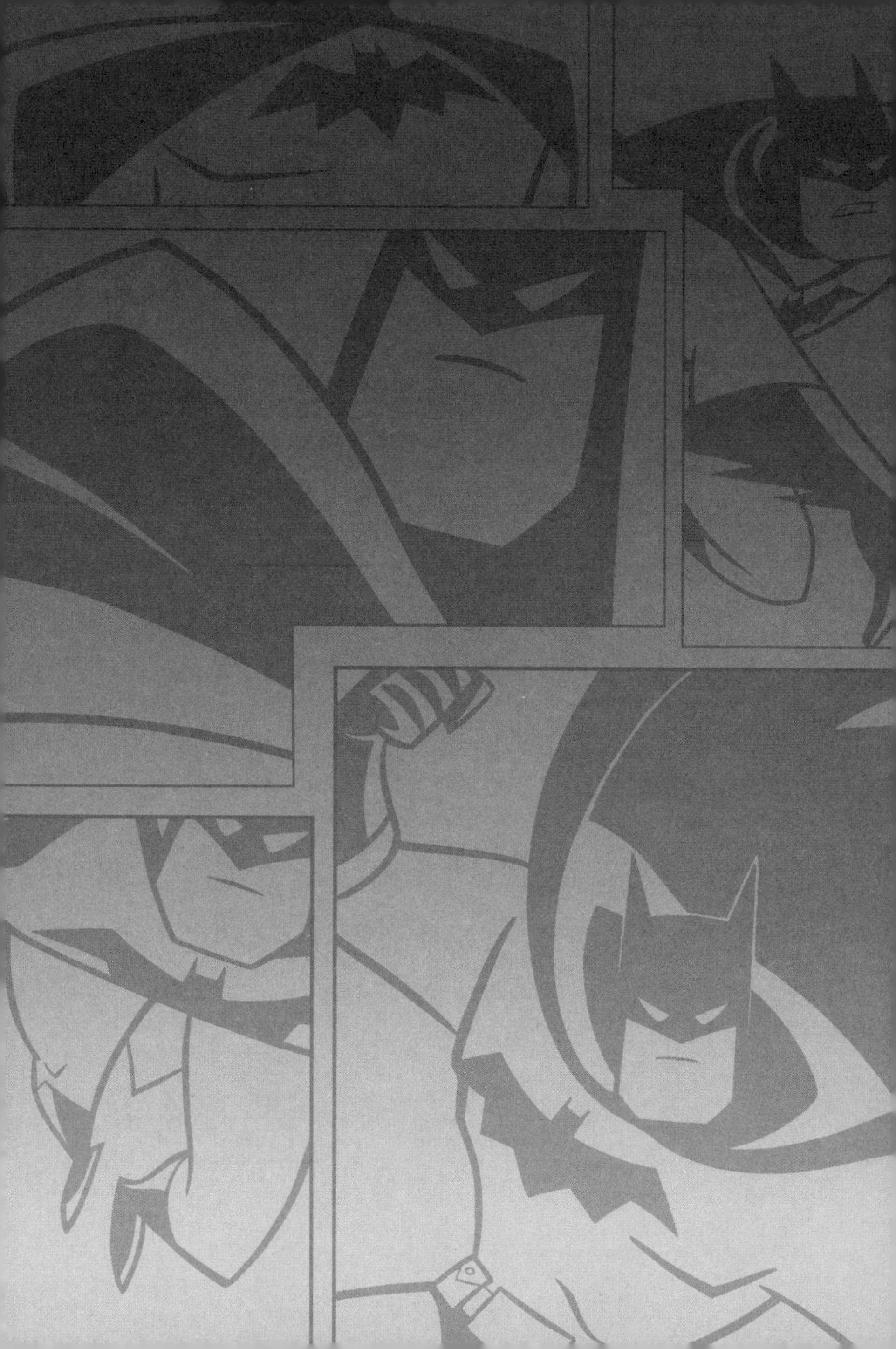

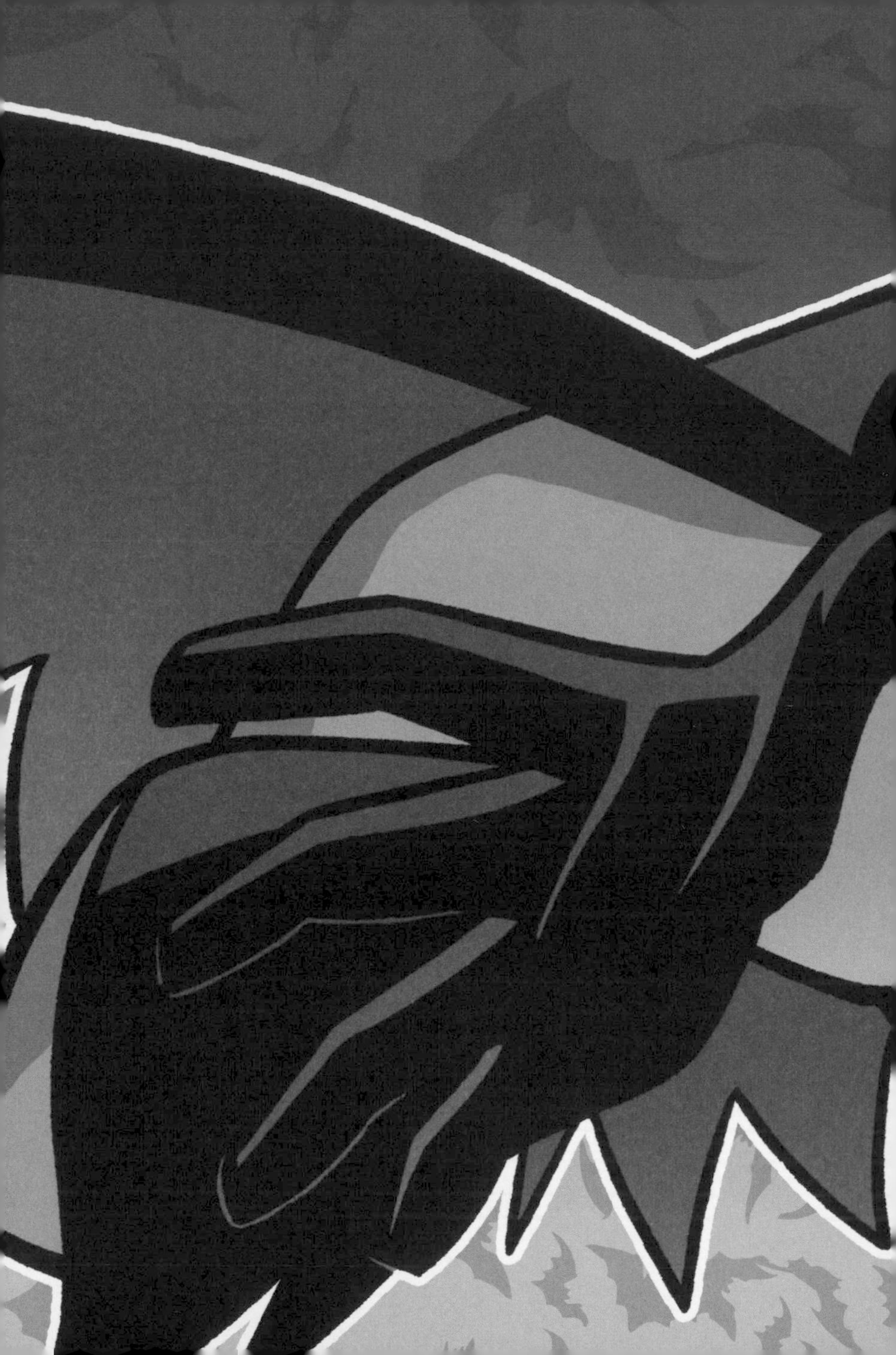

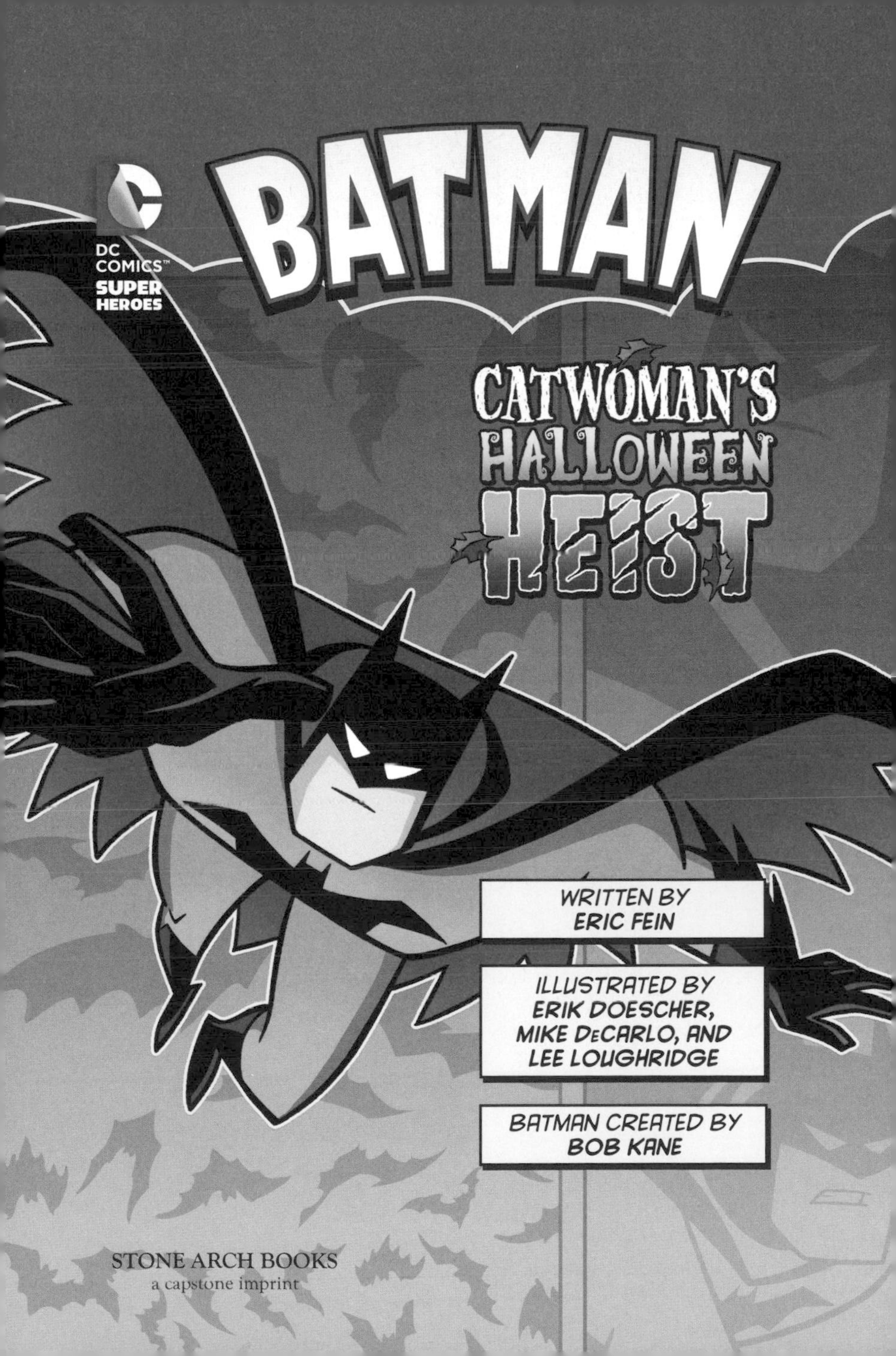

DC COMICS™ SUPER HEROES

BATMAN

CATWOMAN'S HALLOWEEN HEIST

WRITTEN BY
ERIC FEIN

ILLUSTRATED BY
ERIK DOESCHER,
MIKE DECARLO, AND
LEE LOUGHRIDGE

BATMAN CREATED BY
BOB KANE

STONE ARCH BOOKS
a capstone imprint

Published by Stone Arch Books
A Capstone Imprint
1710 Roe Crest Drive
North Mankato, Minnesota 56003
www.capstonepub.com

STAR13131

Cataloging-in-Publication Data is available at the Library of Congress website.

ISBN: 978-1-4342-2132-2 (library binding)
ISBN: 978-1-4342-2767-6 (paperback)

Summary: Barbara Gordon, the secret super hero Batgirl, has been invited
to the biggest Halloween party of year. Unfortunately, she already agreed to
spend the night with Robin, her younger crime-fighting partner. Instead of
arguing with her mentor, Batman, Barbara decides to bring Robin along. That
night, the teens arrive at the costume party, hosted by an eccentric collector
of Halloween artifacts. Suddenly, all of the lights go out! When they turn on,
his prized artifact, a black cat made of rare diamonds, is missing! One of the
masked guests must have stolen it, and Batgirl and Robin must capture the
feline felon.

Art Director: Bob Lentz
Designer: Brann Garvey
Production Specialist: Michelle Biedscheid

Printed in the United States of America in Stevens Point, Wisconsin.
112013
007879R

TABLE OF CONTENTS

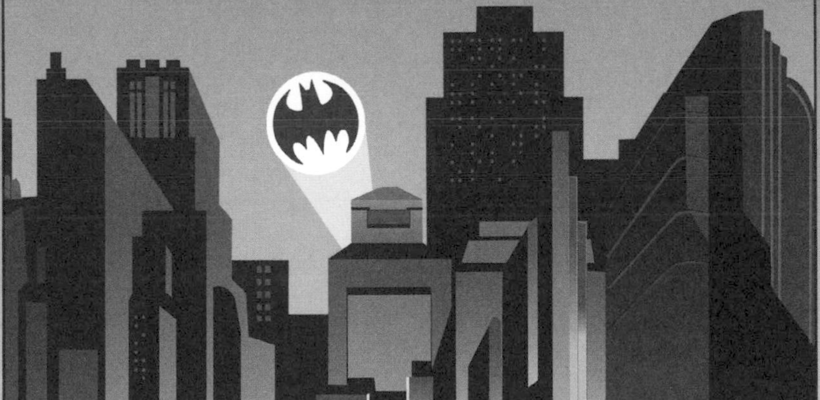

CHAPTER 1

DOUBLE DUTY

On a chilly afternoon, Barbara Gordon ran into the mall in downtown Gotham City. She needed to pick up a few more bags of Halloween candy for the trick-or-treaters that evening. Unfortunately, hundreds of other people had the same idea. As the secret super hero Batgirl, Barbara often battled the world's worst villains — but she wasn't prepared to fight the holiday crowd.

"What a waste of time," Barbara said to herself. She turned and headed toward the mall's exit empty-handed.

"Barbara?" shouted someone behind her. She immediately recognized the voice of Jason Graves, one of her classmates.

Barbara hadn't planned on running into the most popular boy in school. She quickly fixed her hair, checked her breath, and spun around.

"Oh, hi!" said Barbara, acting surprised. "What are you doing at the mall?"

Jason held up several bagfuls of candy and Halloween decorations. "My dad's throwing a costume party tonight," he replied. "He asked me to grab a few last-minute things."

Barbara already knew about the party. According to her friends, it was going to be *the* social event of the year. Unfortunately, she hadn't been invited.

"A costume party?" asked Barbara, pretending she didn't know about it. "That sounds like fun."

"Would you like to come?" asked Jason.

"Really?!" Barbara exclaimed. She tried to hold back her excitement. "I mean, I might be able to stop by later."

"Cool," replied Jason. He swung the shopping bags over his shoulder and headed outside. "Maybe I'll see you there."

"Yeah, maybe," said Barbara. She watched the automatic doors shut behind Jason and then let out a little squeal. "*Definitely*," she whispered to herself.

Moments later, Barbara jumped into her car and called Batman, her crime-fighting mentor. If she planned on going anywhere that night, she needed his permission first.

"Batman?" asked Barbara, speaking into her car's wireless transmitter.

"At your service, Miss Gordon," replied the Dark Knight.

"Very funny," said Barbara. She pulled out of the mall's parking lot and headed toward the interstate. "Where are you?"

"I'm on my way to Arkham Asylum," said Batman. "Apparently, one of the inmates is having a mental breakdown. Nothing too unusual for Halloween."

"About that," said Barbara. "I just got invited to a costume party."

"Halloween is the busiest crime night of the year, Barbara," Batman said. "You and Robin are supposed to patrol the streets."

"I know that," began Barbara, "but maybe he could come with me."

Barbara cringed at bringing Robin, her younger crime-fighting partner, to the party. However, she knew it might be the only way to convince Batman to let her go.

"The party is at the Graves Mansion on the city's east side. We'd be able to keep an eye on one of Gotham's wealthiest neighborhoods," Barbara added. She nervously waited for Batman's response.

"That's not a bad idea," said the Dark Knight. "Just keep in close communication. If either of you see anything suspicious, you know where to reach me."

"Thanks, Batman," said Barbara. "We'll be sure to let you know." **CLICK!** She switched off the computer, turned on her car's afterburners, and sped toward Wayne Manor to pick up the Boy Wonder.

CHAPTER 2

TREATS AND TRICKS

Later that night, Barbara arrived at the Graves Mansion with Tim Drake, the secret identity of Robin. Surrounded by other luxury houses, the dark, frightening mansion looked like something out of an old-time monster movie.

Jason Graves' father, Stephen, owned the mansion. He had made his fortune writing dozens of best-selling horror novels. Each one sold tens of millions of copies all over the world. The money allowed him to live like a king.

Mr. Graves had been a horror buff since he was a kid and had always wanted to live in a haunted house. So when the millionaire couldn't find a real one, he had one built. He nicknamed his creepy home "Halloween House" and filled it with all sorts of Halloween and horror antiques.

"Wow!" Tim said as Barbara parked the car in the Graves' driveway. "What a house! It's bigger than Wayne Manor."

Barbara and Tim got out of the car and walked up to the front door. A sign on the entrance read, "Beware: Killer Party Inside!"

"Ha!" Tim laughed. "That's funny! I like this Jason guy already."

"Please don't embarrass me tonight, Tim," Barbara said. "I mean it." She gave the teen a quick stare and headed inside.

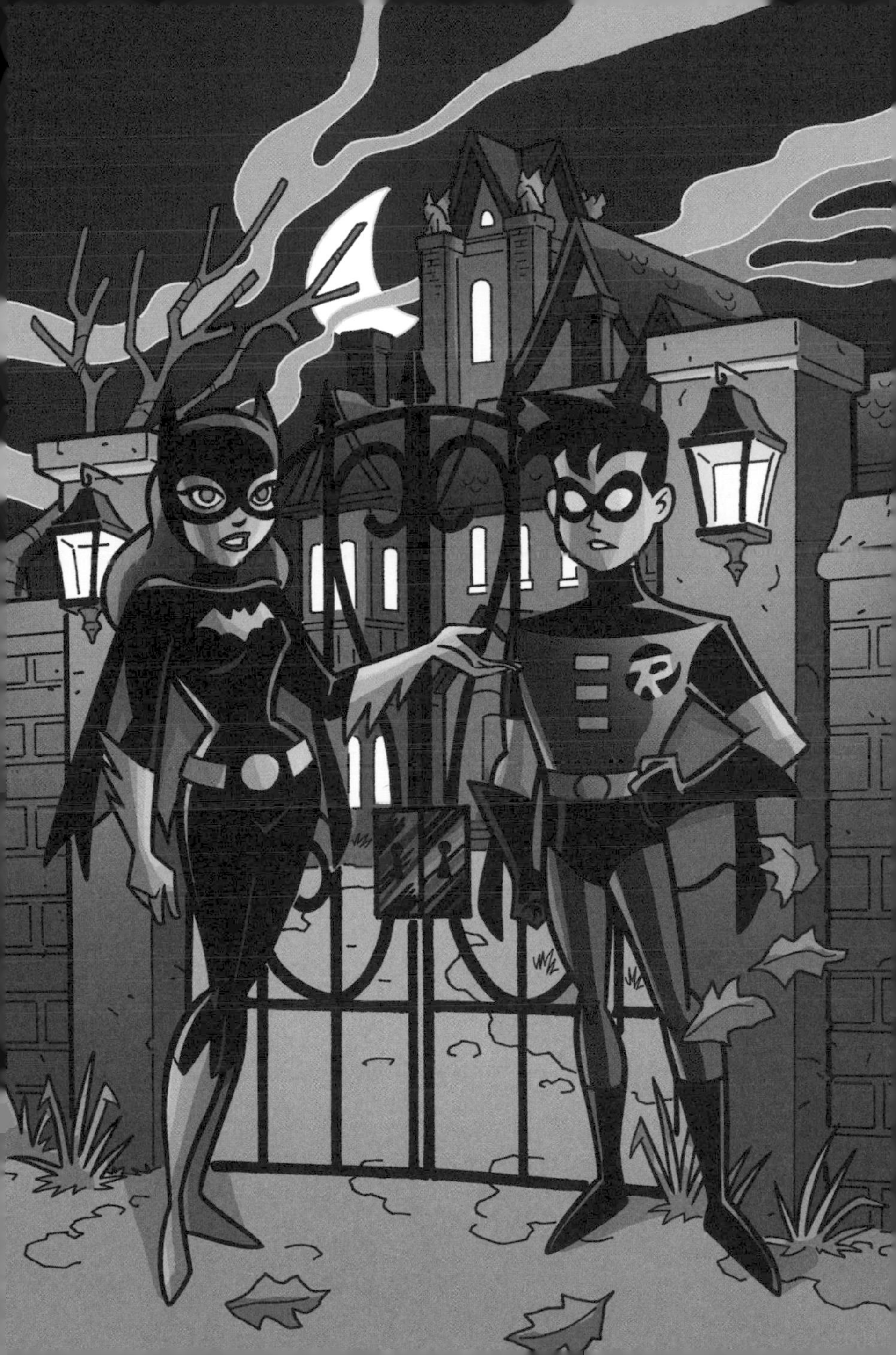

Dozens of people in Halloween costumes packed the mansion. Many were dressed as their favorite super heroes, including Batman, Superman, the Flash, Green Lantern, and Wonder Woman. Several others had dressed as super-villains. The party had three Jokers, two Penguins, three Riddlers, a Mr. Freeze, and four Catwomen. The remaining guests wore costumes of ghosts, witches, and monsters.

Tim and Barbara decided to wear their Batgirl and Robin uniforms as costumes. Halloween was the one time of year that they could dress as their secret identities without drawing attention.

"Nice costume," someone said behind Barbara. She spun around to once again find herself face to face with Jason Graves. He was not wearing a Halloween costume.

"Hi, Jason! It's me. Barbara," she said.

"Wow! I didn't even recognize you," said Jason. "Where did you find that outfit?"

"A, um, friend made it for me," replied Barbara with a smile. "Where's yours?"

"I stopped dressing up when I turned thirteen," he explained. "I think wearing costumes is pretty silly. No offense."

"None taken," said Barbara. "I never would have worn this costume if I wasn't with him." She pointed to Tim, who was already at the buffet table.

"No sweat, Barbara," said Jason. "You'll stop feeling silly once you see my dad's costume. It's completely embarrassing."

CLICK! Then suddenly, the lights in the mansion went out. Several of the guests began to scream. "What's happening?!"

KA-BOOM! A loud clap of thunder echoed through the room. Then the lights came back on, and Stephen Graves was standing at the top of the stairs. He was dressed as Count Dracula.

Barbara pretended to be scared. She leaned into Jason, who put his arm around her. Jason shook his head as his father came down the stairs. *Why does Dad always have to put on a show?* he thought.

"Welcome," shouted Mr. Graves, "to Halloween House! Bwah ha ha!!"

POOF! With a wave of his cape, Mr. Graves disappeared. Then he reappeared on the other side of the room. "Dear guests, there is nothing to fear. It was just a simple trick — one of many you'll experience tonight," he said. "Now come, let me show you my terrifying collections."

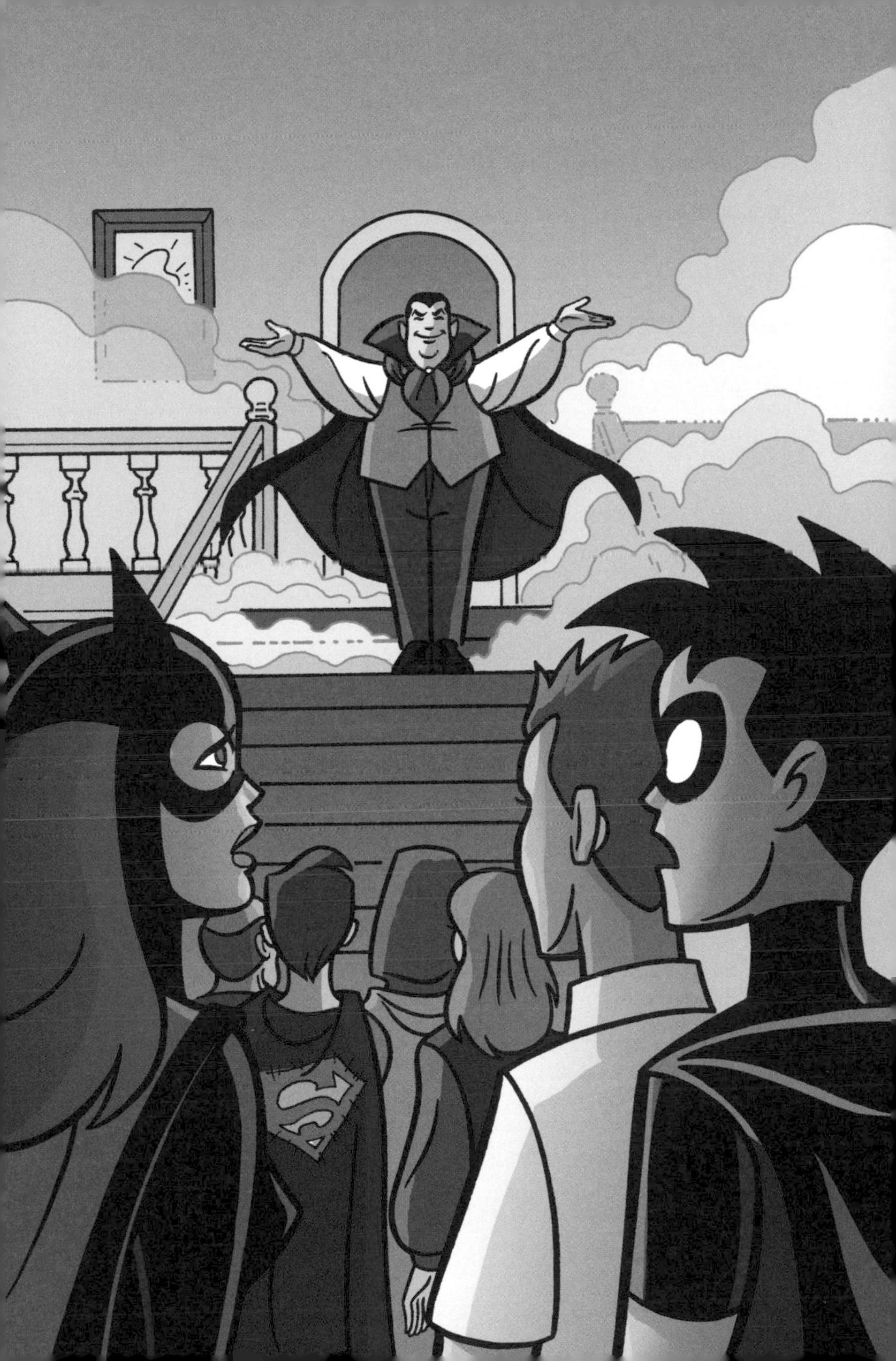

As the other guests followed their host, Barbara and Tim stayed behind. Barbara took out her cell phone and called Batman, as he had instructed.

"Hi, Bruce," she said into the phone.

"Is everything all right?" the Dark Knight replied.

"So far," said Barbara. "It appears Gotham's villains are behaving tonight."

"Let me know if anything changes," said Batman. "I just arrived at Arkham Asylum. Once I investigate the disturbance, I'll be heading back to the Batcave."

* * *

The Dark Knight switched off his mobile communicator. He stepped out of the Batmobile and headed inside the asylum. It was home to Gotham's worst criminals.

At the asylum's front door, two guards in bulletproof vests greeted Batman. "Thank you for coming," said one of the men. He shook the super hero's hand and then quickly took off down the hallway. "Her prison cell is down here."

Batman followed the guards through a darkened corridor, which led to the maximum-security area of the asylum. This area contained the worst of the worst — criminals who would never again see the light of day. As they passed each cell, the sound of someone banging on the floor grew louder and louder.

"Is that her?" asked the Dark Knight.

"Yes, she's been like that all day," replied the guard. "Everyone here is afraid to enter her cell, even though she is in titanium shackles. That's why we called you."

Just then, Batman and the guards arrived at the final prison cell. Through the steel bars, the Dark Knight saw one of his trickiest enemies — Catwoman!

At the moment, however, the feline felon looked more mad than menacing. With her hands shackled to her feet, the villain rolled back and forth on the prison cell floor. She kicked wildly at the ground, trying to break free from her chains.

"Let me in," demanded the Dark Knight.

"But," began one of the guards, "we're not supposed to open —"

"You called me here," Batman said.

The guard pulled out a key, steadied his hand, and placed it in the lock. "We can't be responsible for what happens," he said.

CHAPTER 3

HALLOWEEN HEIST

Back at the Graves Mansion, Barbara and Tim had rejoined the rest of the guests. Mr. Graves was leading them on a tour through the first floor of his mansion.

"Each room of my house is built around historical Halloween objects," continued Mr. Graves. "This room contains my frightening collection of masks. Only the brave of heart should enter here."

Mr. Graves invited them into the room. Dozens of creepy masks decorated the walls. Some were hundreds of years old.

"Scary, aren't they?" said their strange host. "Originally, Halloween masks were worn to frighten away ghosts, not people. My, how times have changed."

In the back of the group, one of the guests raised his hand. "I thought this party was going to have a haunted house?" asked the teen. "This stuff is boring."

"Yeah, Dad," said Jason, sensing his friends were about to leave. "Nobody cares about these silly antiques."

"Oh, really?" replied Mr. Graves. He opened the door to the next room. "Let me show you one last item. It's my favorite, and most valuable, treasure in the house."

Except for a glass display case, the room was completely empty. Inside, sat a sculpture of a sparkling black cat.

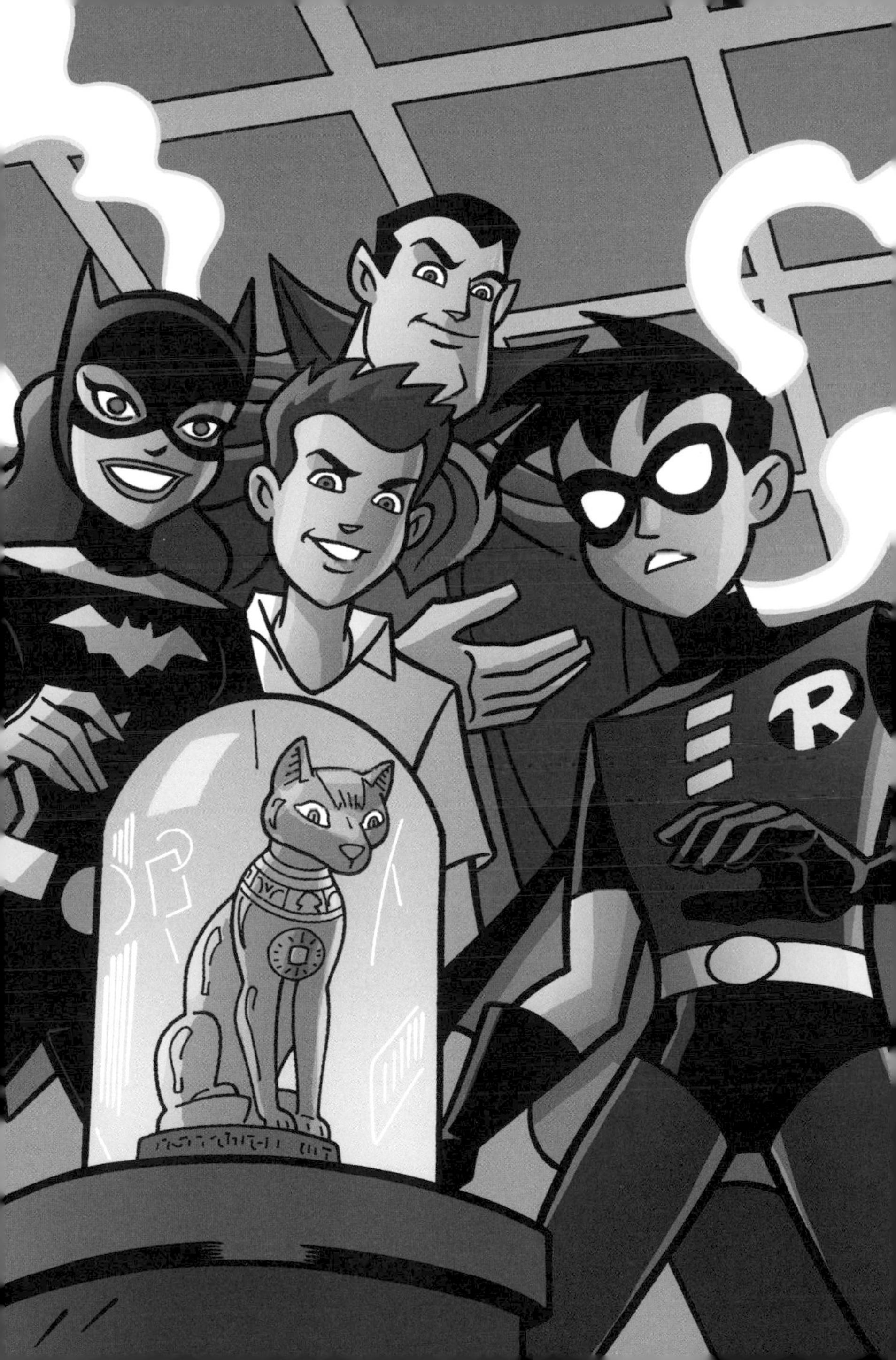

"People all over the world have feared black cats for hundreds of years," said Mr. Graves, standing near the sculpture. "Many people believe that they bring bad luck."

Mr. Graves typed a secret code into the electronic keypad near the display case. "But that's not true," he continued. "This black cat was cut from a rare diamond. And tomorrow, it will bring me nothing but good fortune!"

The display door swung open. Mr. Graves took out the sculpture and held it in the air. "I'm selling this Black Cat Diamond to a private investor for $100 million," he exclaimed.

The guests gasped in amazement.

"Not so silly, huh, Jason?" he said.

*   *   *

Back at the asylum, Batman entered Catwoman's cell. He kneeled next to the villain and removed a lock-picking device from his Utility Belt. He carefully inserted the device into the shackles and turned it.

As the cuffs released from the prisoner's wrists, Batman jumped to his feet. He expected Catwoman to attack with her razor claws. But instead, she stood, walked toward Batman, and gave him a hug.

With her hands free, the woman in the black outfit removed her mask. Instead of Selina Kyle, Catwoman's true identity, Batman saw the face of another woman — a janitor at Arkham Asylum.

"But, but, how —?!" said a prison guard.

"Never underestimate Catwoman," said Batman. "She can escape any situation."

At the costume party, Mr. Graves held the Black Cat Diamond toward his guests. "Take a good look," he said. "You may never see this priceless jewel again —"

Suddenly, the lights went out again!

People screamed and ran in all directions. Tim pushed through the crowd of guests and found the light switch. He quickly turned them back on. **CLICK!**

Everyone was nervous, even Mr. Graves. The host looked down at his hand. "It's gone!" he screamed. "Someone has stolen my Black Cat Diamond!"

The guests stood in shocked silence as Mr. Graves paced the room wildly.

"Come on, Dad," Jason said. "You've had your fun. Put the diamond back in its display, and let's move on."

Mr. Graves looked at his son. His face went pale. "This isn't a joke," he said. "The diamond has been stolen. Someone in this room is a thief!"

Mr. Graves walked over to a wall unit that controlled the security system for the entire house. He pressed a red button on the control panel. In an instant, heavy steel doors came down over all the windows and exits. **THUD!** The house was now completely sealed.

"Until I find the Black Cat Diamond," shouted Mr. Graves, "nobody gets in or out of this house!"

CHAPTER 4

HALLWAY OF HORRORS

Mr. Graves walked among the guests, looking them over from head to toe. He asked each person if they stole the jewel. When nobody confessed, he demanded that everyone empty their pockets, but none of them had the diamond.

For the first time that night, Mr. Graves noticed that Tim was younger than the other kids. "You!" he shouted at Tim. "You're not one of my son's friends!"

"He's with me, Mr. Graves," Barbara said. "I didn't think it would be a problem."

"Ease up, Dad," Jason said. "This is Barbara Gordon, the police commissioner's daughter. She didn't come here to rob you!"

Mr. Graves sighed. "You're right," he said. "Please accept my apology."

"Of course," Barbara replied. "If you let me, sir, I'll help you find the diamond."

"That's kind of you, Barbara," said Mr. Graves, "but everyone should just stay put. This thief could be dangerous."

Barbara realized that Mr. Graves and the other guests didn't know that she was actually Batgirl. Barbara had to find a way to help, without revealing her true identity. She stepped into an empty room and called the Dark Knight.

"Batman," Barbara began. "There's been some trouble at —"

BZZT! After a sudden burst of static, the phone went dead. The steel doors that had secured the house were also blocking all cell phone signals. She and Tim would have to handle this situation on their own.

*   *   *

At Arkham Asylum, Batman hung up his phone and paced back and forth inside Catwoman's cell. *What was Barbara trying to tell me?* he wondered. *She sounded worried.*

The Dark Knight had already gotten the janitor to confess. She admitted that the real Catwoman offered her one million dollars to unlock the cell. The deal turned out to be more than she had bargained for.

Batman spotted a shredded newspaper in a trash can. He picked up several torn sections of the front page.

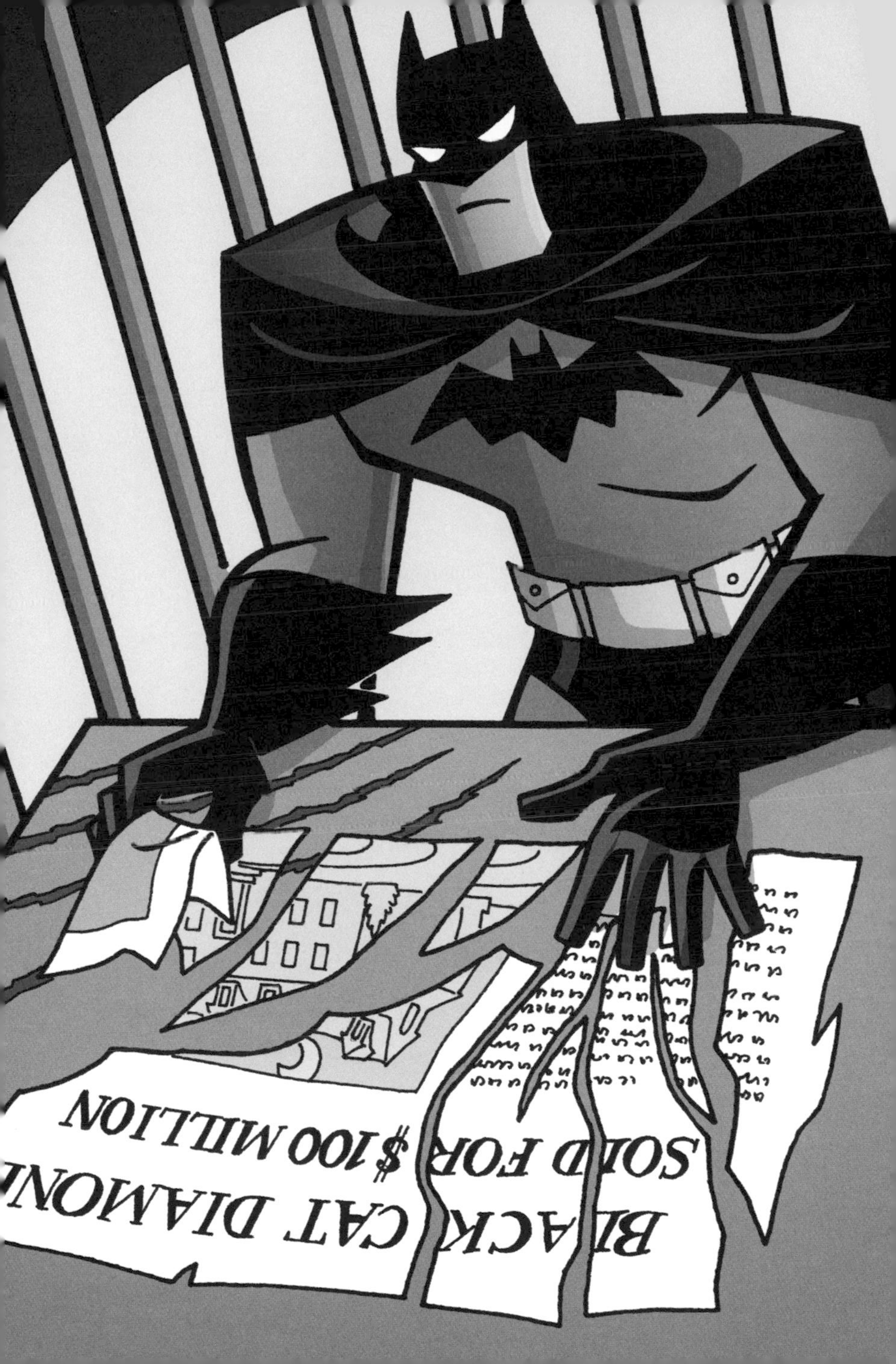
BLACK CAT DIAMON
SOLD FOR $100 MILLION

As the Dark Knight placed each piece of paper on a table, the mystery came together like a puzzle. "$100 million," read one of the pieces. "Black Cat Diamond," read another.

Then Batman looked at the final piece. "Stephen Graves," he said to himself.

FLAP! Batman threw down the newspaper and raced out of the room. He had a costume party to crash.

*   *   *

Meanwhile at the Graves Mansion, Tim studied the other guests. Something about the crowd was bothering the teenage super hero. He silently counted the people standing in the room.

"Hey, one of the cats is missing!" Tim suddenly shouted.

"Of course, the Black Cat is missing, genius," another teenager said. "Why do you think we're locked in here?"

"What does he know?" said a boy in a Batman costume. "He's only a sidekick!"

Several of the guests chuckled. They didn't know Tim was the real Robin.

"You're not listening!" shouted Tim. "There used to be four girls in Catwoman costumes. Now, there are only three."

Mr. Graves looked around. "He's right!" he said. "You don't think —?"

"Look!" Tim exclaimed. He pointed toward a wooden banister, which led up a tall staircase. "Claw marks!"

"Wait here! I'm calling the police!" said Mr. Graves. "She's probably still in the house somewhere."

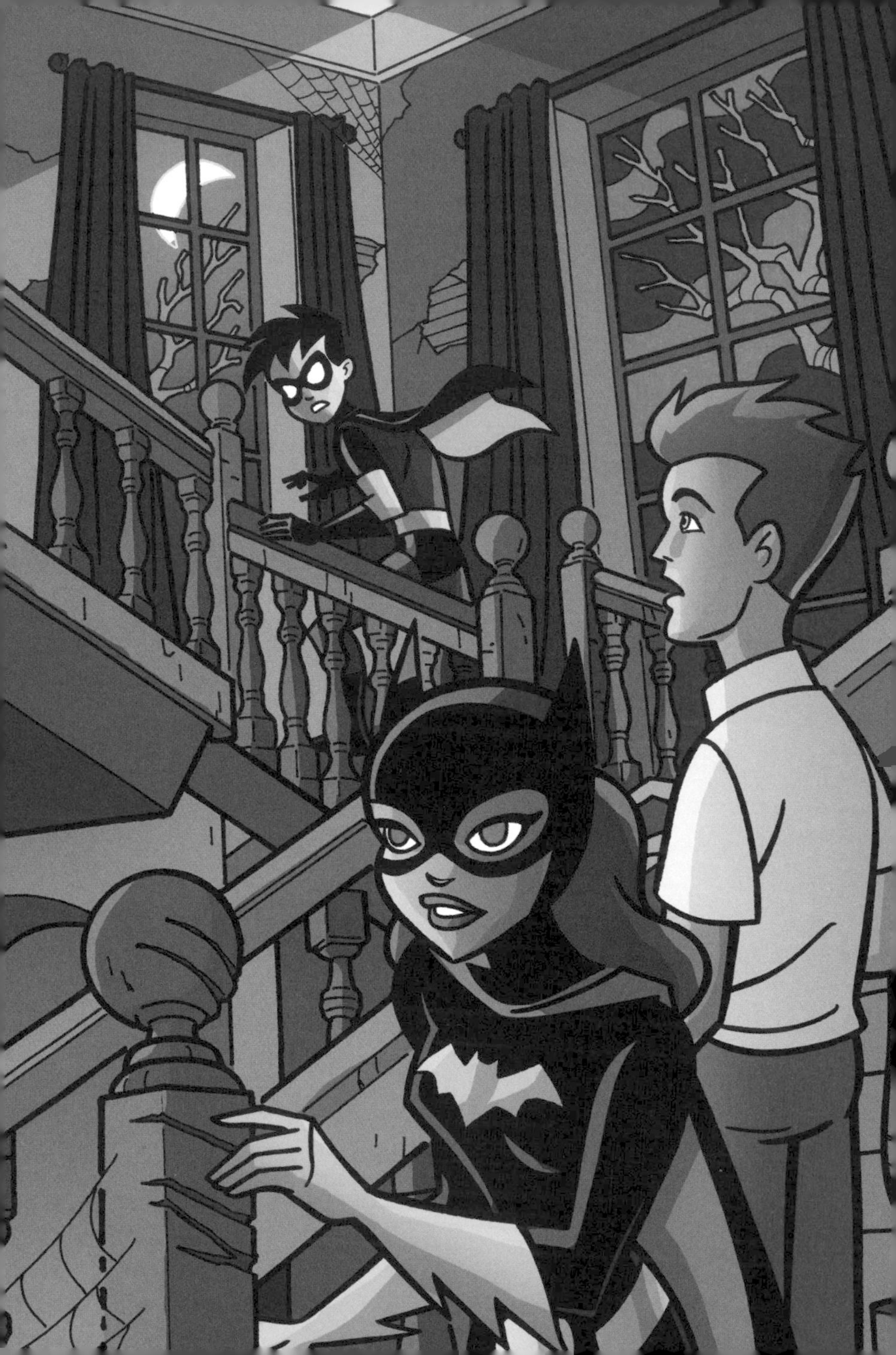

Tim had taken on Catwoman before. He knew that she would be long gone by the time the police arrived.

"We have to search the house before she can escape," Tim said to Barbara and Jason as he ran ahead of them up the stairs.

"No!" Jason said. He grabbed Barbara by the arm to stop her from going up. "Stay behind me. I'll protect you."

Barbara allowed Jason to go in front of her. She could barely hide her smile. *That's cute,* she thought. *He thinks I need protecting. If he only knew . . .*

At the top of the stairs, Barbara and Jason caught up to Tim. The floor had thirteen doors — six on the left side and six on the right. On the final door, at the end of the hall, glowed the number thirteen.

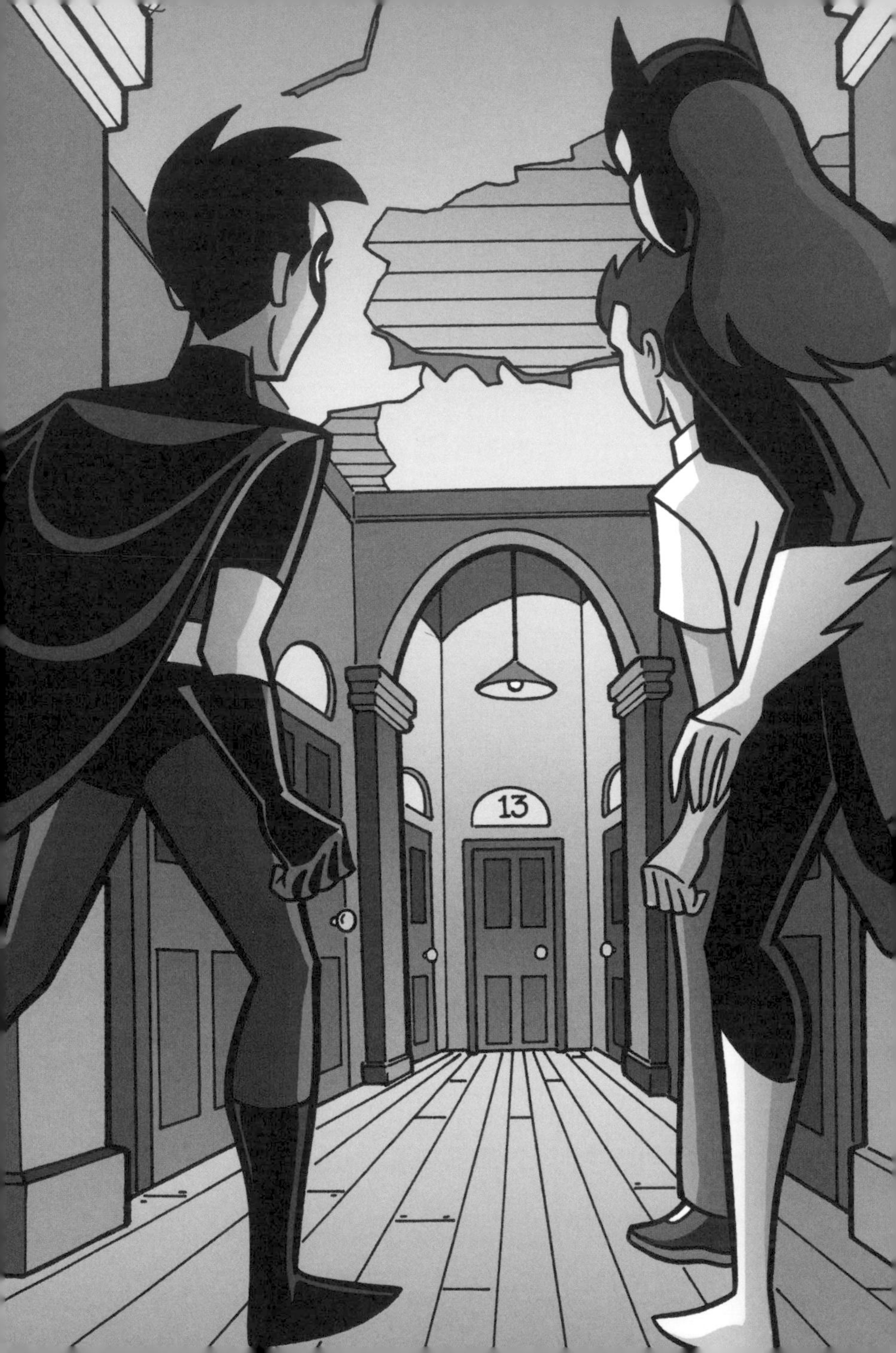
13

"Oh, great," said Jason, looking down the creepy hallway. "I almost forgot about my dad's Thirteen Doors of Terror!"

"Thirteen what?" asked Barbara.

"This is my dad's famous haunted house," replied Jason. "He's rigged these rooms with some of the scariest special effects on Earth. It'll be impossible to find Catwoman in here."

Nearby, Tim crouched at the keyhole to the door closest to the stairs. He was trying to pick the lock.

"What are you doing, Tim?" Barbara said. "Didn't you hear Jason? We need to figure out a plan."

"Come on, Barbara," said Tim. "I'm not scared of a few cardboard skeletons and some fake cobwebs. Follow me!"

Tim stood up and opened the door. He stepped inside the darkened room. Suddenly, a giant bat dropped down from the ceiling and soared toward his head.

SQUEAK! SQUEAK! SQUEAK!

"Ah!" Tim shouted. He quickly bolted out of the room. "What is that thing?!"

Jason reached up and plucked the bat out of the air. He threw the creature onto the ground, lifted his foot, and stomped down hard. **SMASH!** The electronic bat exploded beneath his shoe.

"Sorry about that," Jason said. "I told you that my dad likes to surprise people. He's always adding things to his collection. I never know what I'll find when I open a door in this house."

"Thanks for the warning," Tim said.

The Boy Wonder went through the next door, and Barbara and Jason followed. They searched each room on the floor, discovering robotic ghosts, mummies, werewolves, and other frightening props.

At the twelfth door, Tim paused for a moment. "Only two doors left," he said. "She has to be here somewhere." Then the secret super hero stepped inside.

WHOOOOSH! Tim watched two hands slash across his chest. "Ha!" he laughed. "I know this is fake, but that felt pretty real."

"Um, Tim," said Barbara, pointing at his chest.

Tim looked down and saw claw marks on his Robin uniform. When he looked back up, Catwoman was standing right in front of him!

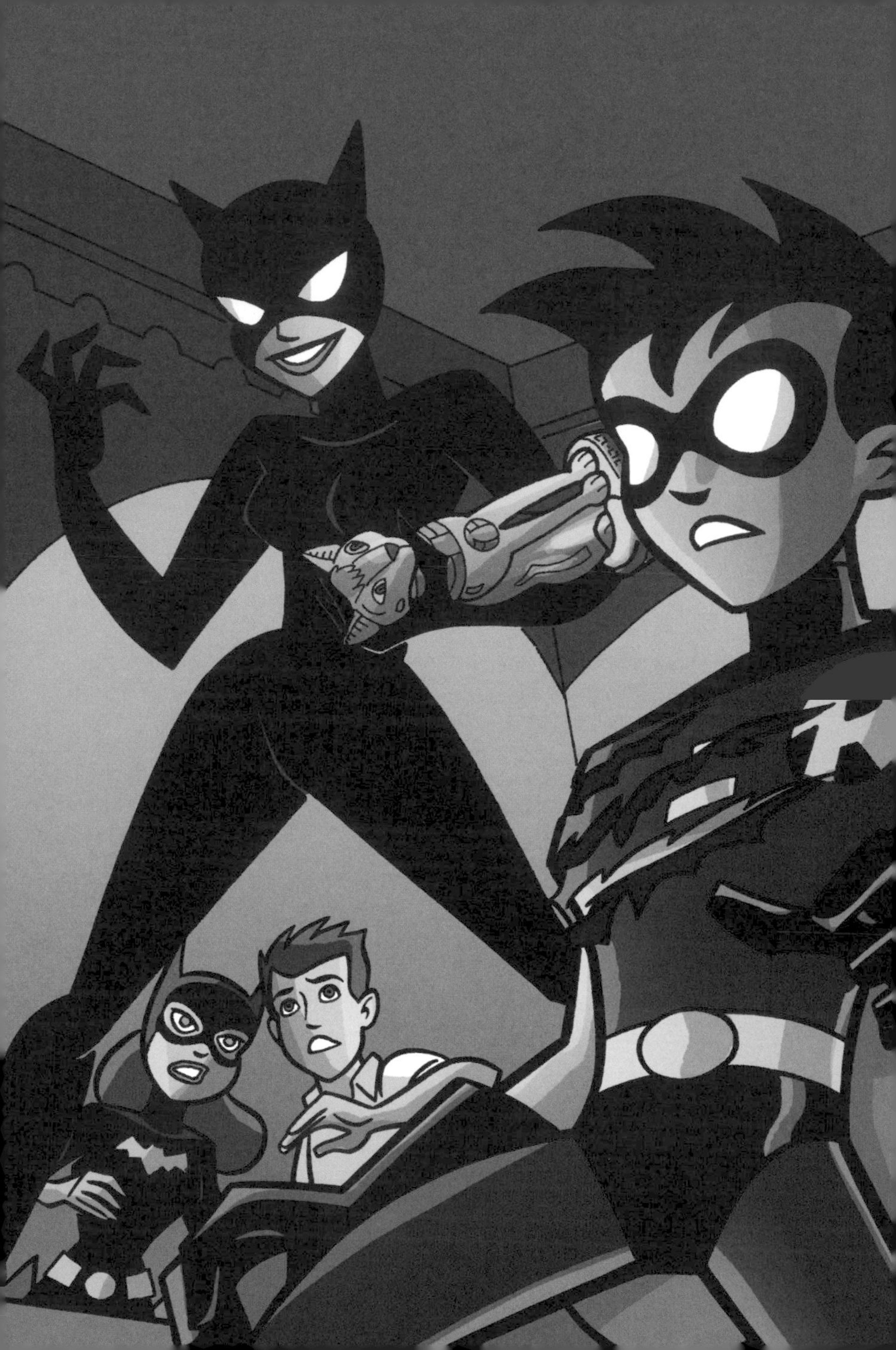

CHAPTER 5

CAT CAPTURE

Catwoman swiped her claws at Barbara. Then she ran out of the door and quickly headed down the hallway. Before the teens could reach her, the villain slipped inside the thirteenth door.

"Where does this lead?" asked Tim. He opened the thirteenth door and looked up a tall flight of stairs.

"To the roof," Jason replied. "My dad sometimes writes his books up there when the weather is nice."

The trio raced up the stairs. When they reached the top, Tim was the first one outside, and he quickly spotted Catwoman at the edge of the roof. She was gripping a ladder that led to a dark helicopter overhead.

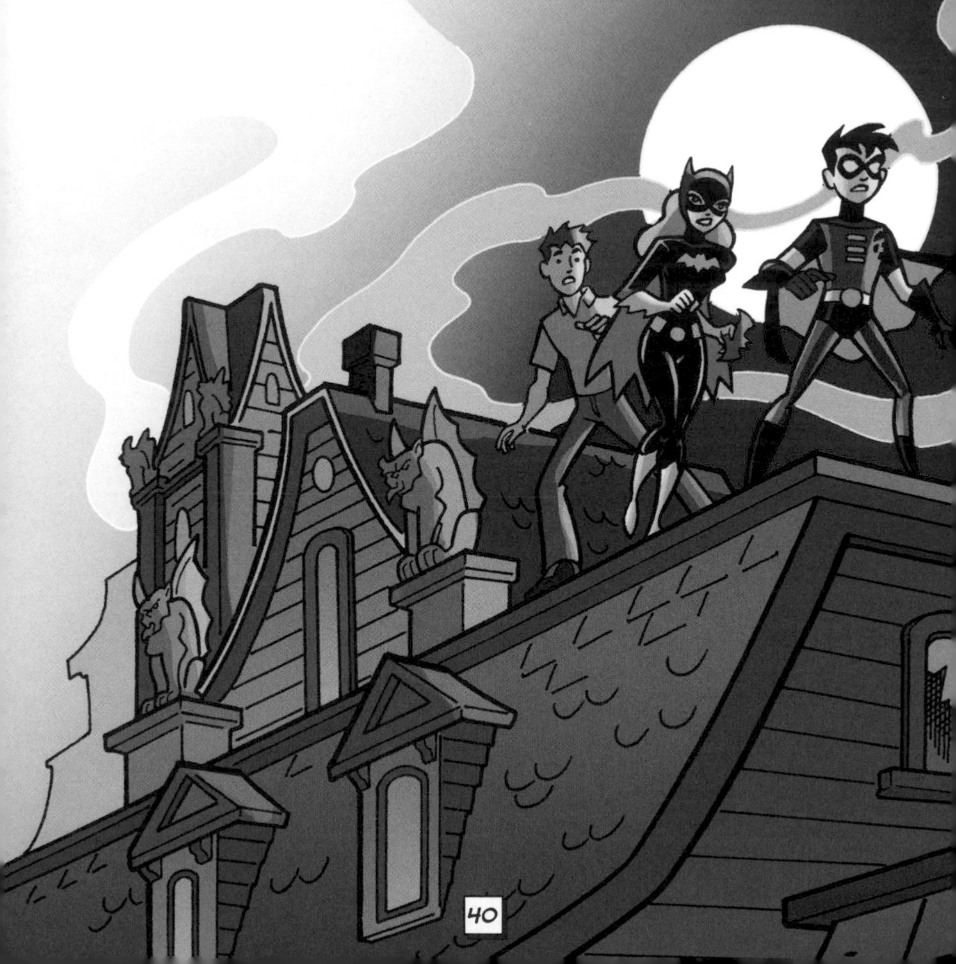

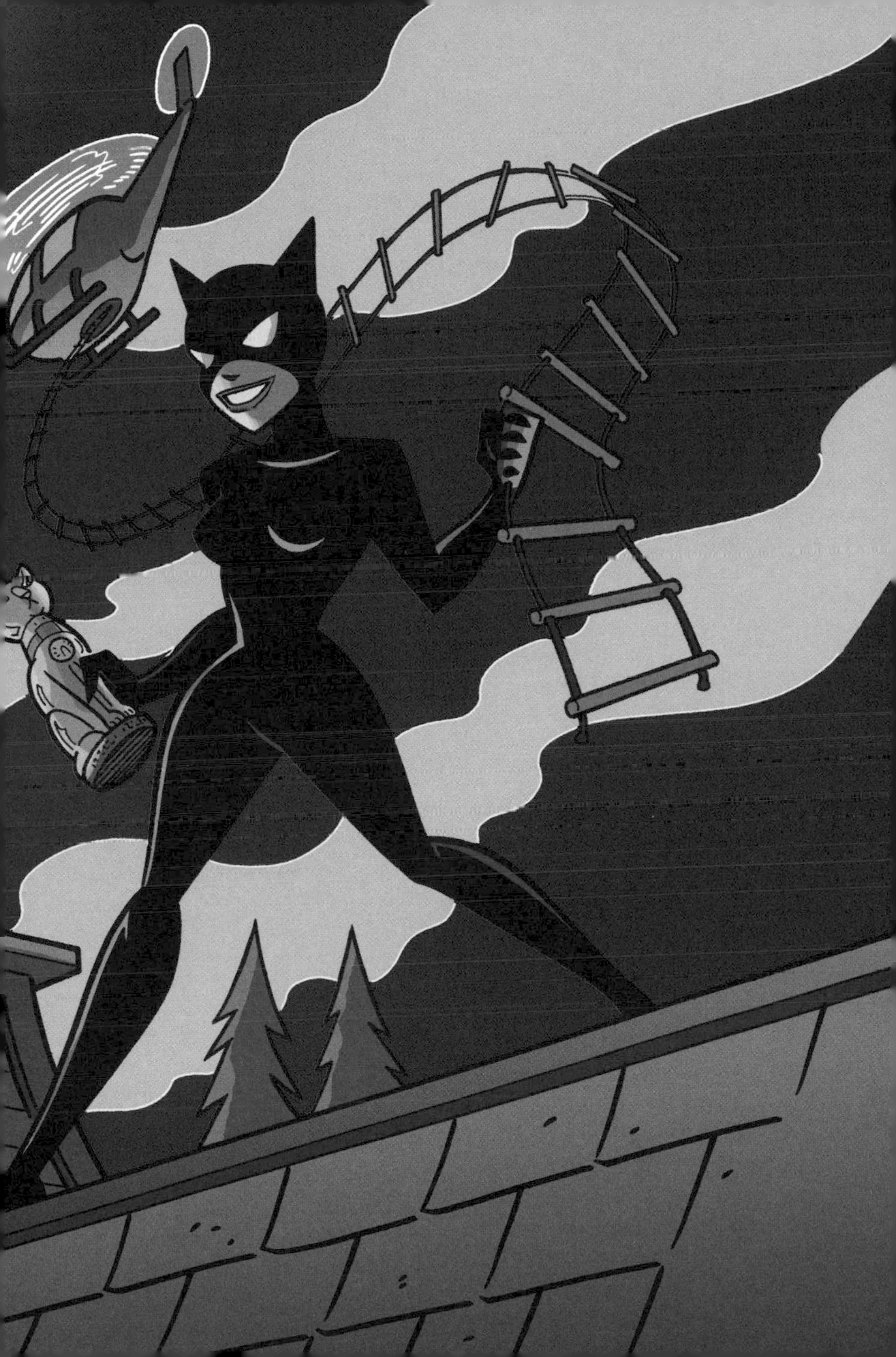

Tim wasted no time. With a flick of his wrist, he threw a Batarang at the escaping villain. Its edge sliced through the ladder's cables. **ZING!** Catwoman's means of escape collapsed in a pile at her feet.

"That's some costume!" Jason exclaimed. "You'd think Tim was the *real* Robin."

As the helicopter flew off, Catwoman quickly came after Tim. The angry feline slashed at him with her razor-sharp claws.

When Barbara went to help, Jason jumped in front of her. "I'll handle this," he said, striding toward the super-villain.

"If you're trying to be a hero," shouted Catwoman, "you're a little underdressed."

"I may not have a silly costume, but I won't let you steal from my dad," said Jason. "Give me the Black Cat Diamond!"

Barbara knew Jason was out of his league. Catwoman would have him for dinner. She watched as Jason made a fist. "Give me the diamond," he said again, "or I'll knock your block off!"

"Try it," Catwoman said.

Jason gritted his teeth. He wound up and threw his best punch.

Before his fist could connect, Barbara quickly took action. She grabbed a Batarang from her Utility Belt, aimed, and flung the weapon at her foe. Catwoman and Jason were so focused on each other that neither of them noticed the Batarang flying their way.

TWANNNGG! The weapon struck Catwoman and knocked her to the ground.

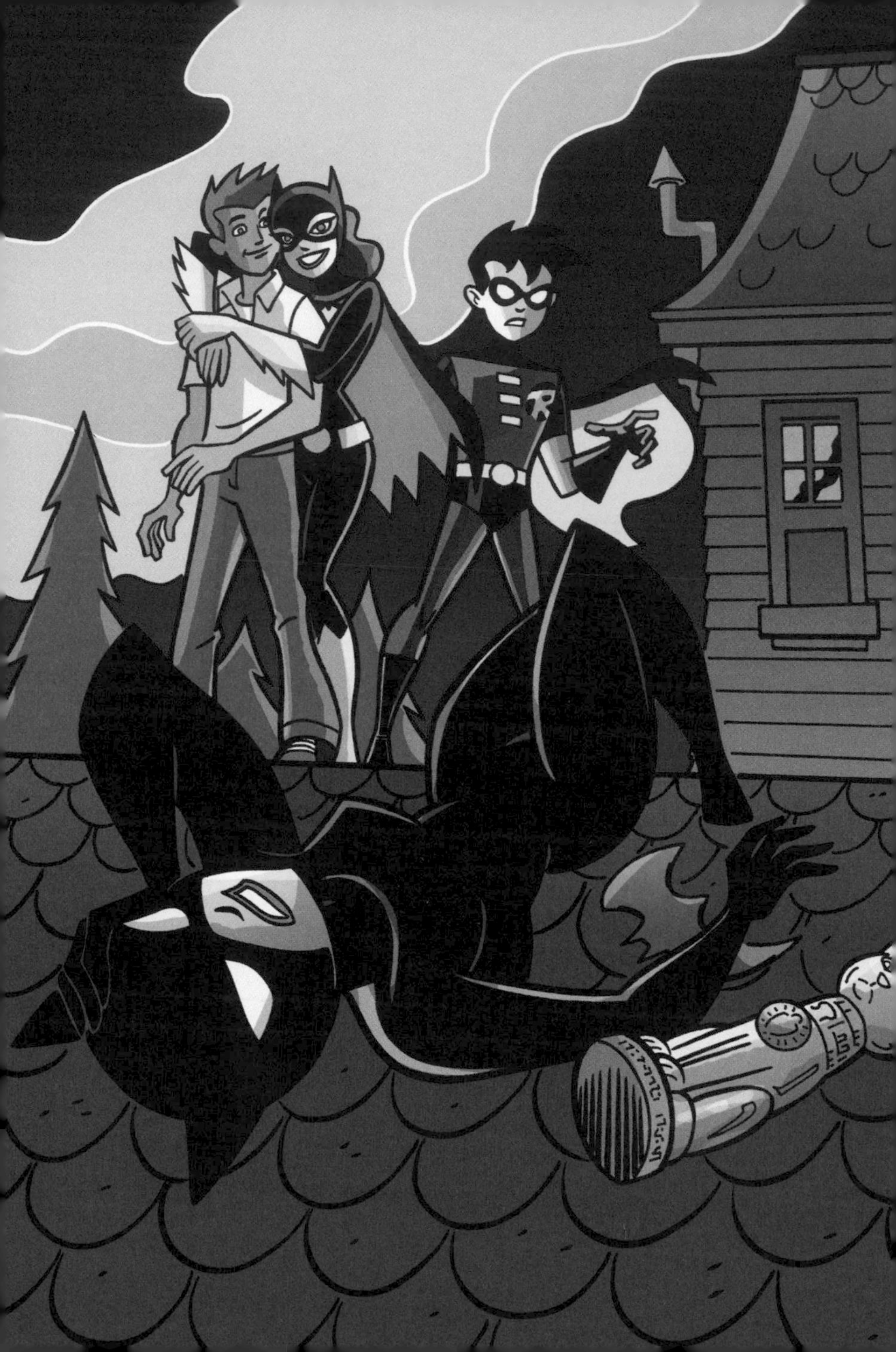

Jason's fist met empty air. He spun around, off balance, and fell on top of the downed Catwoman. **THUD!**

"You did it, Jason!" Barbara said. She ran toward the teenager's side. "Good job."

"Oh, brother," Tim exclaimed.

By the time they brought Catwoman downstairs, the police had arrived. The officers put the Black Cat Diamond into a plastic bag for evidence.

"Take care of that," Mr. Graves said to the officers. "I almost lost a fortune to that crazy woman!"

"Crazy!" yelled Catwoman. "I was going sell the diamond and give the profits to the city's pet shelters. You're a millionaire, but you want to sell the Cat for money. That's what I call crazy!"

Catwoman hissed and continued, "It was a perfect plan. I would have gotten away with it, if it wasn't for those super hero wannabes."

"And thanks to them," said the police officer, "you'll be going back to jail for a long time. But first," he added, "Batman wanted us to double-check something."

The police officer grabbed the villain's mask and yanked it off her head. "Selina Kyle," he said, confirming the identity of the real Catwoman. The officer turned to the teens. "You can never be too sure who's behind the mask on Halloween."

"That's what I love about this night," said Stephen Graves. "On Halloween, you can pretend to be whoever you want."

"We should help the cops," said Barbara.

"Yeah," Tim said. "Let's lend a hand."

"Thanks again, kids," said Mr. Graves. "The *real* Batgirl and Robin couldn't have handled it any better."

Barbara and Tim each gave a little smile. Then they dusted off their uniforms and started to say their good-byes.

"By the way, those costumes are just like the real thing," Mr. Graves said. "I need to have them for my collection. Where did you get them?"

"Dad," Jason said with a groan. "No more collectables. Please."

*   *   *

On the roof of a nearby house, the Dark Knight crouched in the shadows. His black cape flapped in the cool breeze.

Batman had arrived in time to see Batgirl and Robin defeat Catwoman on the roof of the Graves Mansion. The teens had managed to capture the feline felon without revealing their own secret identities.

Quite a trick, Batman thought. Though Batgirl and Robin were still young, they had become full-fledged heroes.

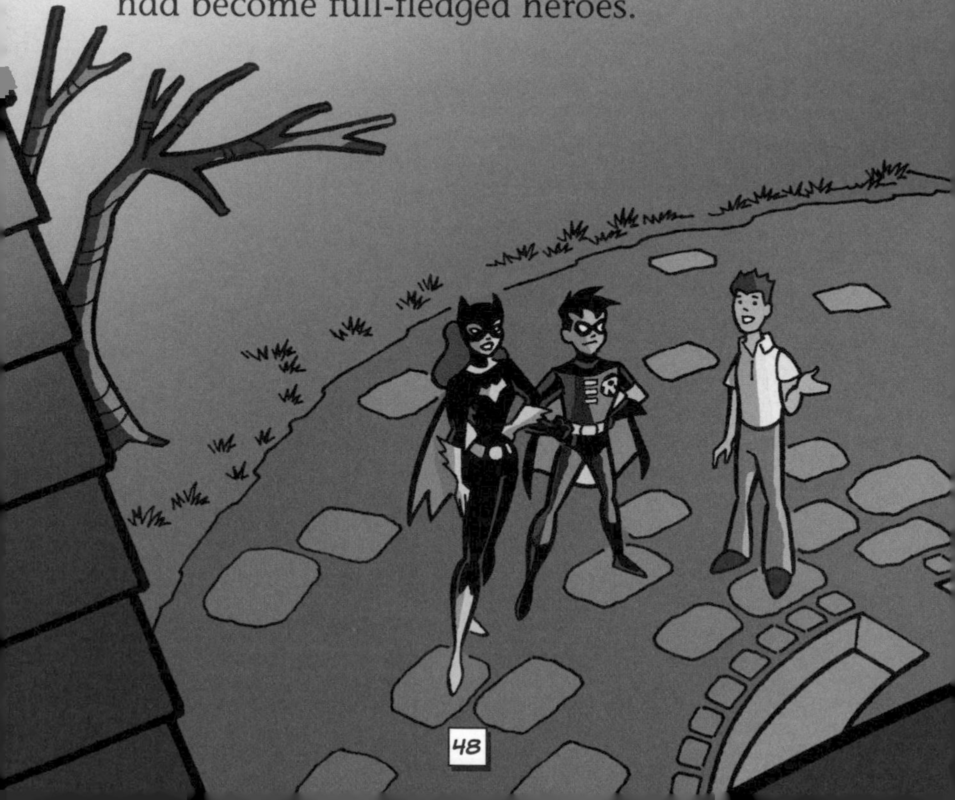

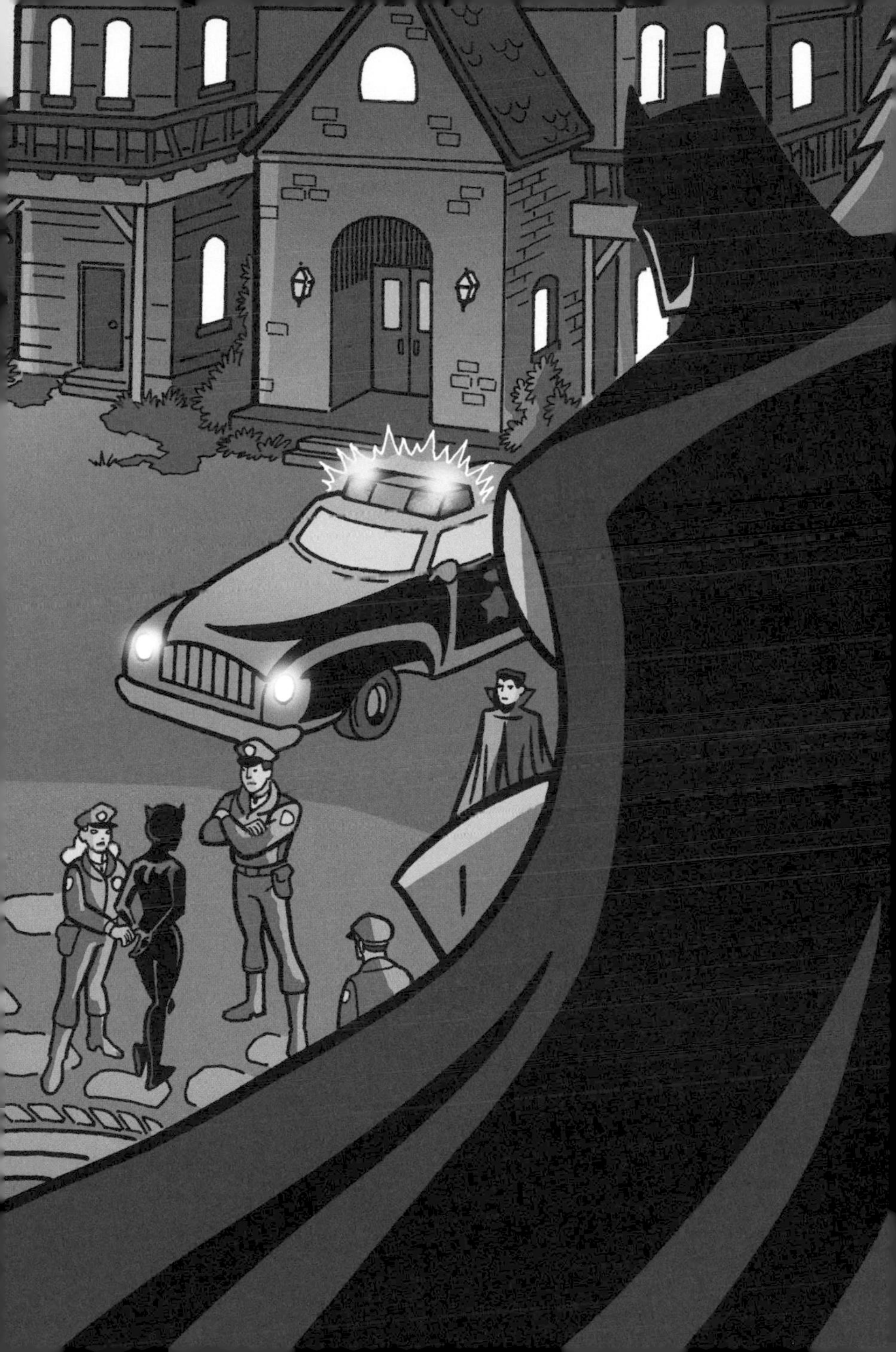

Catwoman

REAL NAME: Selina Kyle

OCCUPATION: Professional Thief

BASE: Gotham City

HEIGHT:
5 feet 7 inches

WEIGHT:
125 pounds

EYES:
Green

HAIR:
Black

Like Bruce Wayne, Selina Kyle was orphaned at a young age. But unlike Bruce, Selina had no caretakers or family fortune to support her. Growing up alone on the mean streets of Gotham, Selina was forced to resort to petty crime in order to survive. She soon became one of the city's most dangerous criminals. Becoming Catwoman to hide her true identity, Selina prowls the streets of Gotham, preying on the wealthy while guarding Gotham's fellow castaways.

G.C.P.D. GOTHAM CITY POLICE DEPARTMENT

- Selina's love of felines led her to choose a cat-related nickname. In fact, much of her stolen loot has been donated to cat-saving charities throughout the world.

- The athletic Selina prefers to use her feline grace and cat-like agility to evade her would-be captors. But when push comes to shove, Catwoman can use her retractable claws to keep her opponents at a distance.

- Catwoman may be a wanted criminal, but she also holds an interest in Gotham's orphans. The money from many of her high-profile crimes has gone to the city's orphanages.

- Selina has been an ally to Batman on several occasions. When a deadly plague spread through the city of Gotham, Catwoman teamed up with the Caped Crusader to help find a cure. However, their alliances never last, since Selina seems uninterested in putting an end to her thieving ways.

CONFIDENTIAL

BIOGRAPHIES

Eric Fein is a freelance writer and editor. He has written dozens of comic book stories featuring The Punisher, Spider-Man, Iron Man, Conan, and even Godzilla. He has also written more than forty books and graphic novels for educational publishers. As an editor, Eric has worked on books featuring Spider-Man, Venom, and Batman, as well as several storybooks, coloring and activity books, and how-to-draw books.

Erik Doescher is a freelance illustrator and video game designer based in Dallas, Texas. He attended the School of Visual Arts in New York City. Erik illustrated for a number of comic studios throughout the 1990s and then moved to Texas to pursue video game development and design. However, he has not completely given up on illustrating his favorite comic book characters.

Mike DeCarlo is a longtime contributor of comic art whose range extends from Batman and Iron Man to Bugs Bunny and Scooby-Doo. He resides in Connecticut with his wife and four children.

GLOSSARY

antiques (an-TEEKZ)—old objects that are valuable because they are rare or beautiful

asylum (uh-SYE-luhm)—a hospital or jail for the mentally ill

Batarang (BAT-uh-rang)—a metal, bat-shaped object that is thrown as a weapon or tool

buff (BUHF)—someone who collects, or knows a lot about, something specific

corridor (KOR-uh-dur)—a long hallway

cringed (KRINJD)—shrank or flinched in fear

full-fledged (FUHL-FLEJD)—of full rank or standing

menacing (MEN-iss-ing)—threatening, intimidating, or dangerous

mentor (MEN-tor)—a wise teacher or role model

titanium (ty-TAY-nee-uhm)—a silver colored, very hard kind of metal

villain (VIL-uhn)—a wicked or evil person

DISCUSSION QUESTIONS

1. Stephen Graves collects priceless antiques. Do you collect anything? Discuss your collections.

2. Batman trusts Batgirl and Robin. Do your parents or teachers trust you? Why or why not?

3. This book has ten illustrations inside it. Which illustration was your favorite? Why?

WRITING PROMPTS

1. Batgirl and Robin hide their secret identities during a Halloween party. Have you ever hidden something from someone? What was your secret? Did anyone find out? Write about it.

2. Catwoman is a master escape artist. Write about her next escape. How does she get out of Arkham Asylum? What tricks or tools does she use? How does Batman catch her? You decide.

3. Imagine that you are throwing the ultimate Halloween party. Write about the activities you'd have, the music you'd play, the food you'd serve, and the people you'd invite!

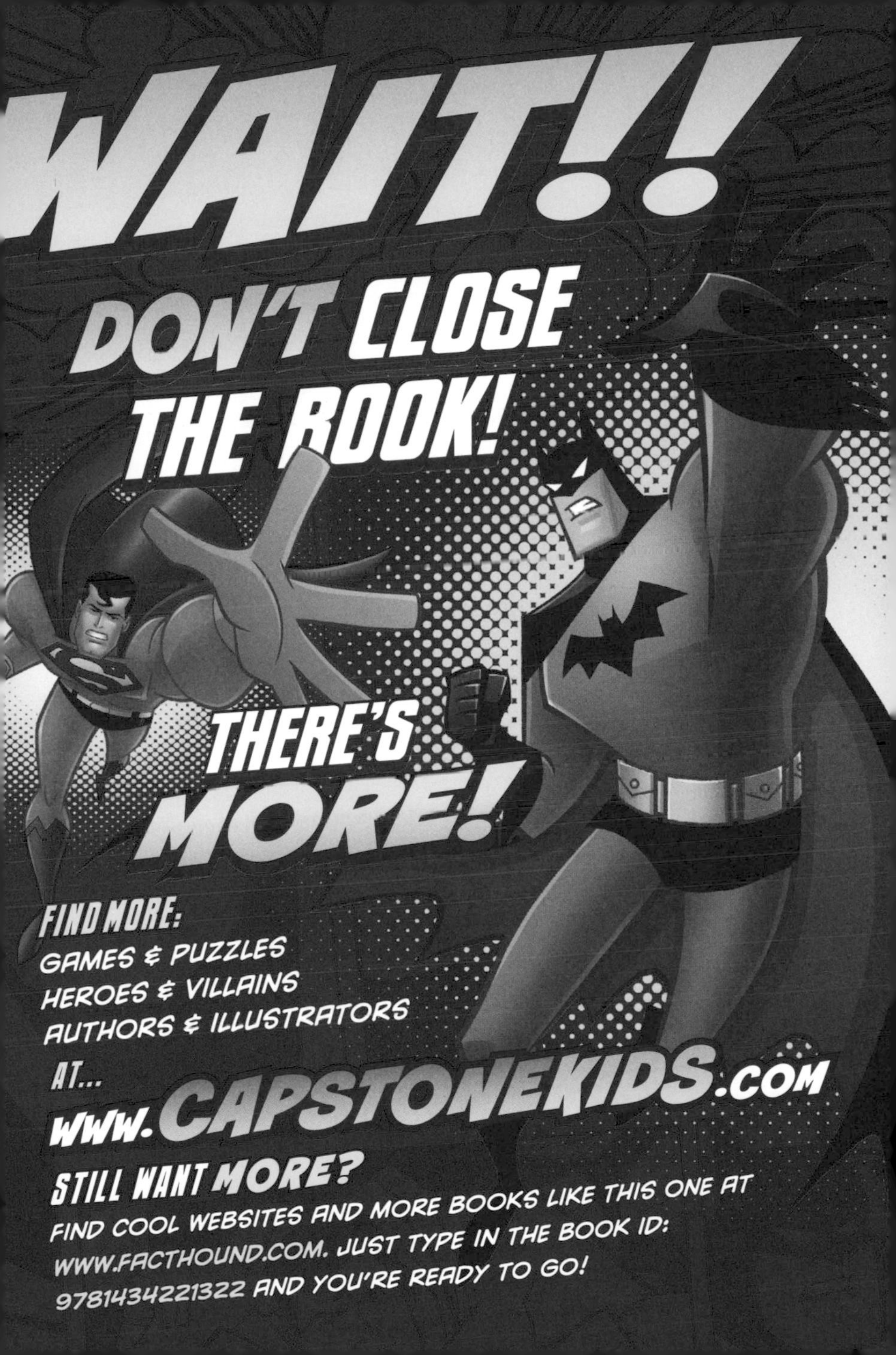
WAIT!!
DON'T CLOSE THE BOOK!
THERE'S MORE!
FIND MORE:
GAMES & PUZZLES
HEROES & VILLAINS
AUTHORS & ILLUSTRATORS
AT...
WWW.CAPSTONEKIDS.COM
STILL WANT MORE?
FIND COOL WEBSITES AND MORE BOOKS LIKE THIS ONE AT
WWW.FACTHOUND.COM. JUST TYPE IN THE BOOK ID:
9781434221322 AND YOU'RE READY TO GO!

MORE NEW BATMAN ADVENTURES!

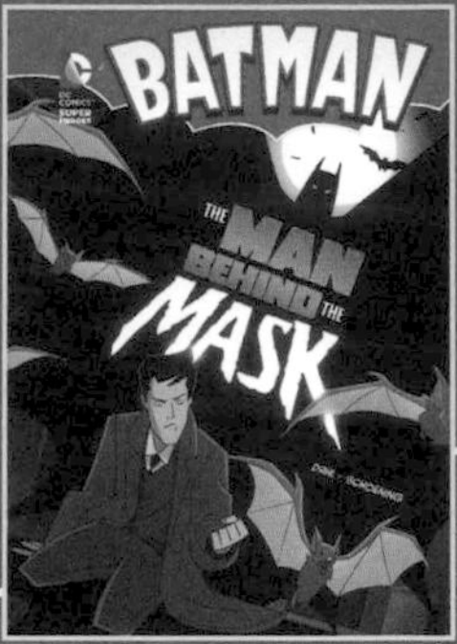
BATMAN
THE MAN BEHIND THE MASK

THE MAN BEHIND THE MASK

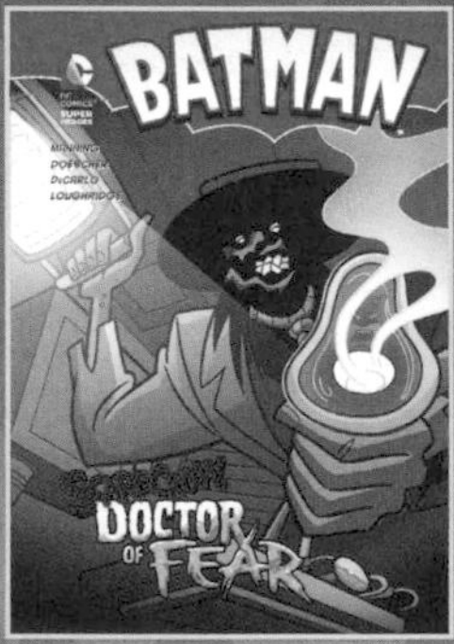
BATMAN
DOCTOR OF FEAR

SCARECROW, DOCTOR OF FEAR

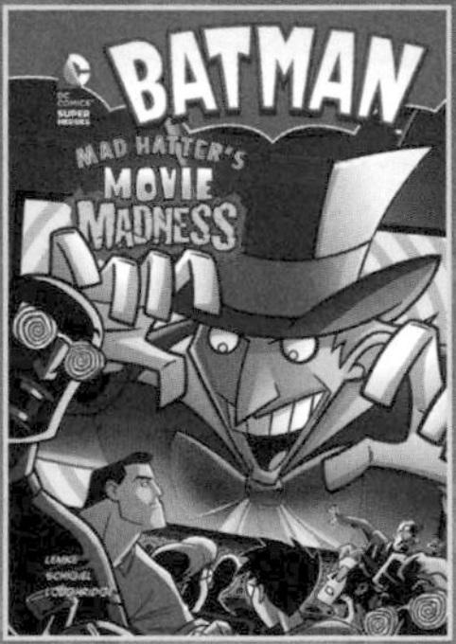
BATMAN
MAD HATTER'S MOVIE MADNESS

MAD HATTER'S MOVIE MADNESS

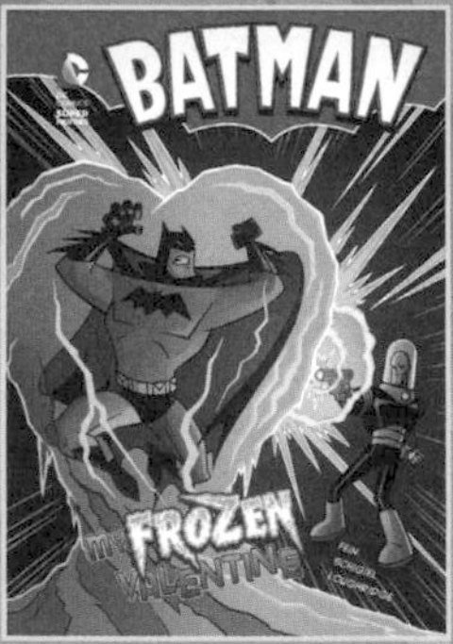
BATMAN
FROZEN
VALENTINE

MY FROZEN VALENTINE

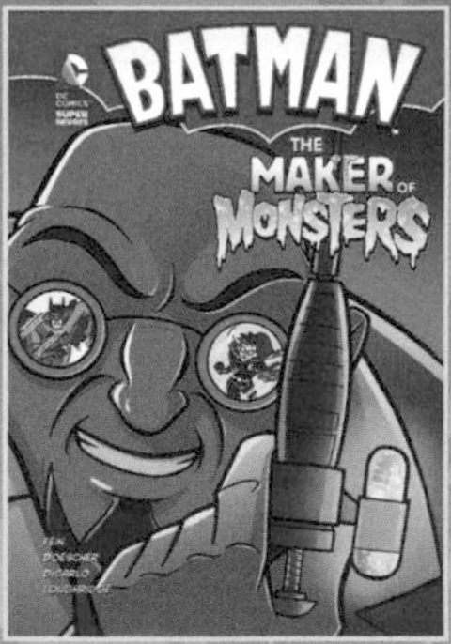
BATMAN
THE MAKER OF MONSTERS

THE MAKER OF MONSTERS

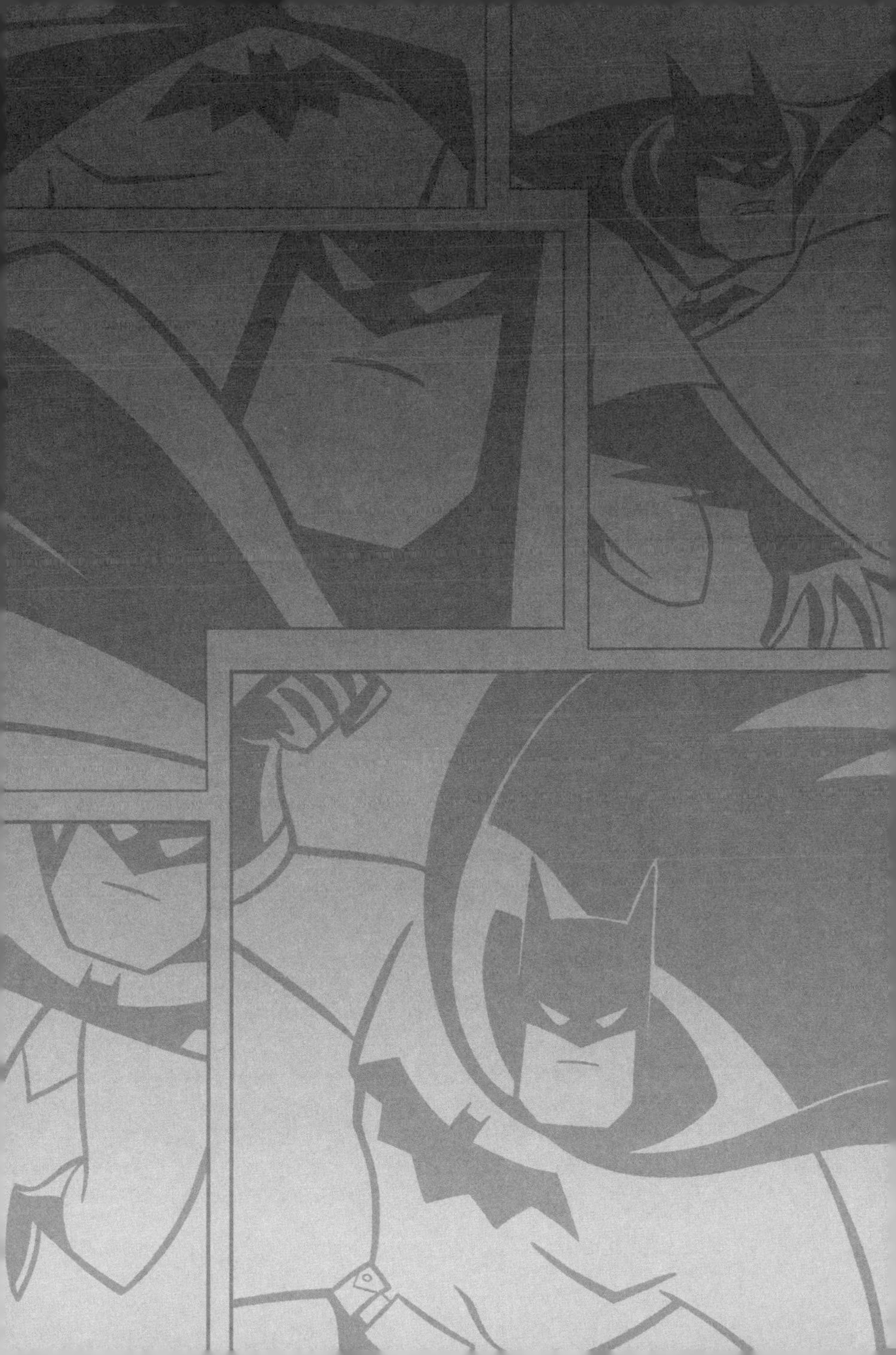

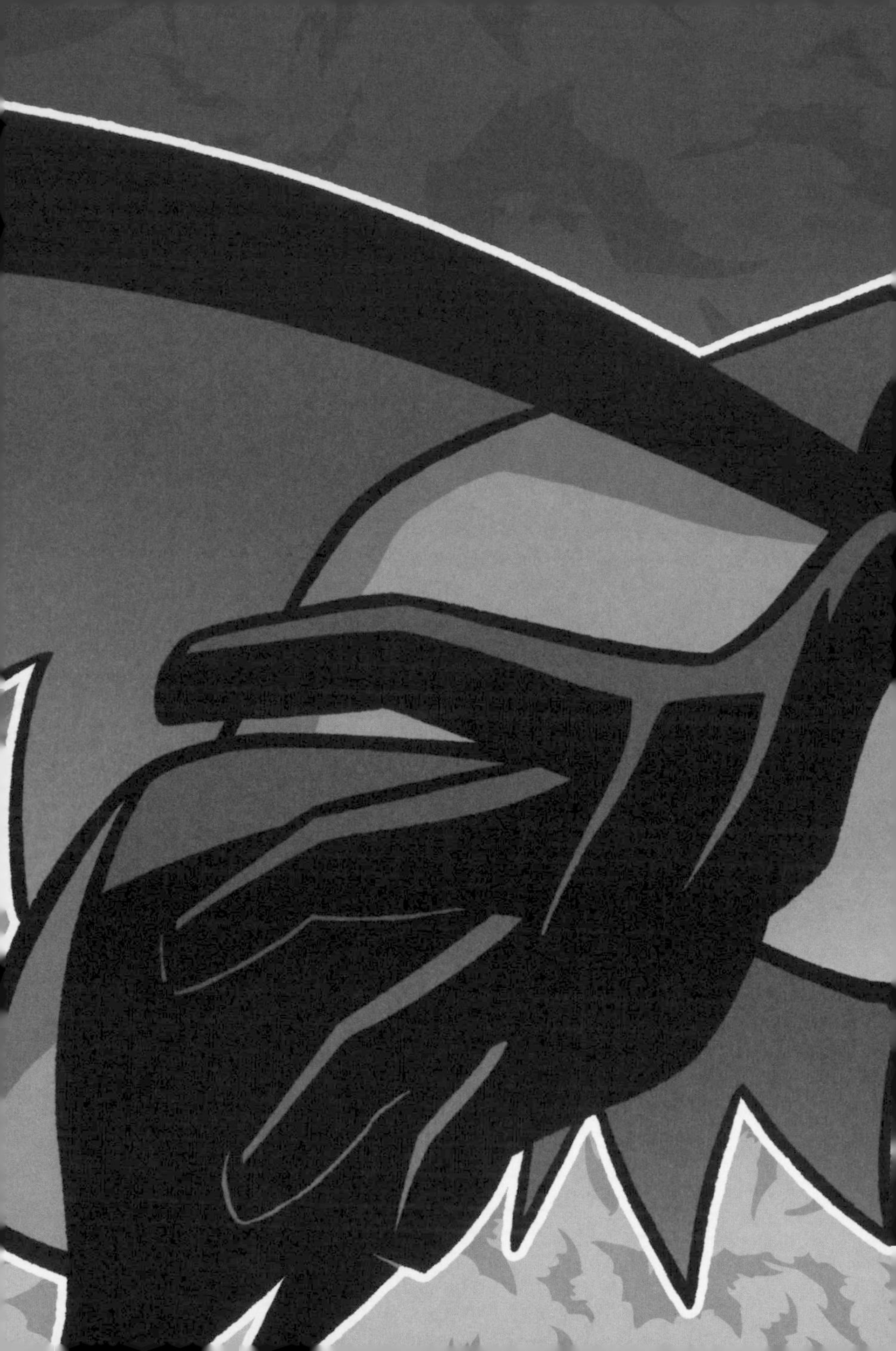

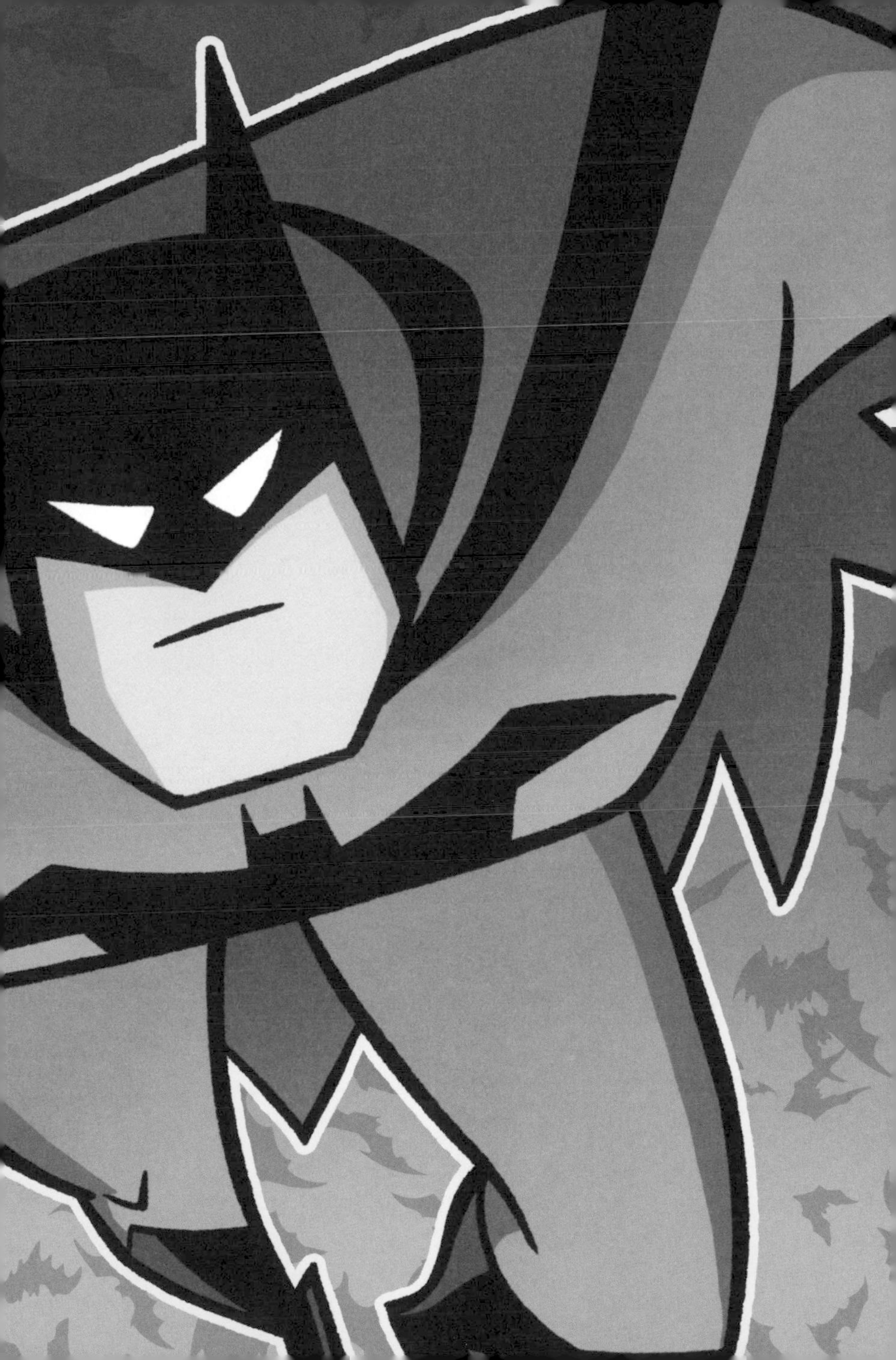